With special thanks to Saji Qorqmaz in Syria, whose help made this book possible.
Also thanks to Syeda Basarat Kazim in Pakistan, Basma Nady in Australia
and Bob Tyrrell of Orca Book Publishers.
—MR

◆

Cataloguing in Publication information available from Library and Archives Canada
ISBN 978-1-4598-1490-5 (bound)

First published in the United States, 2016
Library of Congress Control Number: 2016941573

Summary: In this dual-language picture book (English and Arabic), a young girl and her family are forced to flee
their once-peaceful village to escape the civil war and make their way toward safety in Europe.

Orca Book Publishers is dedicated to preserving the environment and has printed this book on Forest Stewardship Council® certified paper.

Orca Book Publishers gratefully acknowledges the support for its publishing programs provided by the following agencies:
the Government of Canada through the Canada Book Fund and the Canada Council for the Arts, and the Province of
British Columbia through the BC Arts Council and the Book Publishing Tax Credit.

Artwork created using hand-laid stones and photography.
Translation into Arabic by Falah Raheem.
Orca Book Publishers thanks the Inter-Cultural Association of Greater Victoria for their assistance.

Cover and interior artwork by Nizar Ali Badr
Photo of Margriet Ruurs by Kees Ruurs • All other photos © Nizar Ali Badr
Design by Teresa Bubela

ORCA BOOK PUBLISHERS
www.orcabook.com

Printed and bound in Canada.

19 18 17 16 • 4 3 2 1

حَصى الطُرُقات

STEPPING STONES

A Refugee Family's Journey

رحلة عائلة لاجئة

MARGRIET RUURS

تأليف: مارغريت رنرز

❖

ARTWORK BY NIZAR ALI BADR

رسوم: نزار علي بدر

ORCA BOOK PUBLISHERS

Peace cannot be kept by force; it can only be achieved by understanding.
—ALBERT EINSTEIN

◆ FOREWORD ◆

So many stories and interesting pictures are shared online by people all over the world. One day while I was browsing on Facebook, a single image caught my eye. It was a beautiful, tender image of a mother holding her baby. Behind her, the father was trudging along under a heavy load. The image displayed such strong emotion. It touched me deeply. But the amazing thing was the medium. The image was not painted; it was not drawn. It was composed entirely of stones.

Wait a minute, I thought. How can stones display such emotion? Who is the artist who can breathe such life into solid rock?

I looked more closely and noticed that one of the stones was signed: *Nizar Ali Badr.* I searched the name and found a Facebook page full of his amazing work. Each image told a story expressing love, anguish, sorrow or joy. I learned that Nizar was a Syrian, and it soon became evident that much of his work was inspired by the war that has engulfed his country.

Like everyone else, I was familiar with the refugee stories coming out of the Middle East. For many months I had seen and heard the almost-daily news reports of people struggling to cross borders to safety. Of people frantically trying to cross the Mediterranean Sea in unsafe boats, many not making it. Few of us have not been touched by stories of desperate refugees from Syria and elsewhere seeking asylum in the West.

Nizar's work spoke to me strongly. In his art I saw people changing—from happy, carefree children into people burdened and fleeing. There was hurt and sorrow. But ultimately there was also love and caring. And, amazingly, all of this told with stones.

As a children's author, I found myself inspired to create a story that could be illustrated by the art of Nizar Ali Badr. But, of course, I knew I couldn't just use his images without his permission. Artists must be compensated for their creative work. And would Nizar Ali Badr be willing to work with a children's writer he had never heard of from halfway across the world?

There was only one way to find out. But how to contact a stranger in war-torn Syria? So the adventure began. First I sent Nizar Facebook messages. This went on for some time, but to no avail. It occurred to me that perhaps he did not speak English. I wrote him a letter and asked a friend of mine in Australia to translate it into Arabic for me. Again no reply. What if something had happened to him? What if he had fled Syria?

But when I saw a recent Facebook post by him, I knew he was alive. I then asked a friend in Pakistan to see if she could contact him. She soon reported that his Facebook page had reached its friends limit. As a result, he was not getting my messages. Now what? My friend in Pakistan finally managed to get a message through to Nizar in Syria. "My friend Margriet in Canada wants to talk to you," she told him.

"Tell her to email my friend Saji," Nizar replied. "He speaks English."

I was so excited to hear this!

Quickly I sent a message to Saji, who, like Nizar, lives in Latakia, Syria. I explained my idea about making a book together. Would Nizar be willing to let me use his images? Did he still have the original photos? Was the quality of the images high enough for book production?

"Maybe," said Saji.

Saji explained that Nizar, like so many artists, is not a wealthy man. That he collects rocks on the beach for his works. That he does not even have money to buy the glue that would give permanence to his art. Saji explained that after taking a photo of a piece, Nizar often has to take it apart again. I was thrilled when Nizar agreed to work with me on the book.

Next I wondered who would publish a book for which I had the art but was still writing the text. This is not the way children's picture books are typically produced. Also, I wanted a portion of the proceeds from the sale of the book to be donated to an organization or organizations devoted to helping refugees. No one ever gets rich from producing books. Would a publishing house be willing to cut its profits and donate to this cause?

Luck was still with me. I phoned Bob Tyrrell, the founder and president of Orca Book Publishers, and described my vision for the project to him. "Yes," he said immediately, "we'll do it." It turned out that Bob and his wife, Avril, were already involved with a group sponsoring a Syrian refugee family, so he felt the decision was easy for him.

And so we all joined forces, and my plan fell into place. Contracts were signed, advances paid. The book began to evolve into something more than a vision. Nizar created new pieces. Saji translated my questions and took photos of Nizar's art. I wrote and Bob edited. We rewrote and retook photos.

And now we can share our story with you! I hope it will help raise awareness of the plight of those who have to flee the horrors of war. But I hope it conveys too a sense of peace and love, of people helping one another. I am also happy to have played a part in bringing the work of the wonderful artist Nizar Ali Badr to an audience he might not otherwise have reached. This has been an interesting and intriguing project for me… my own journey of discovery. May it be the same for you.

"Rama, wake up!"

the rooster crowed
every morning when we still lived at home.

From my warm bed
I listened as Mama prepared breakfast—
bread, yogurt, juicy red tomatoes
from our garden.

كل صباح عندما كنا نعيش في بلادنا كان الديك يصيح:
"راما، انهضي!"
كنت أصغي من فراشي الدافئ
لأمي وهي تعد الفطور:
خبز، لبن رائب، وطماطم حمراء ريانة
من حديقتنا.

When I was little, not so long ago,
my brother, Sami, our friends and I
played on sunbaked soil.
We laughed, ran across rocks and sand,
free as birds.

When Papa came in from the fields,
he would sit for a time under the orange tree
and tell stories of our ancestors.

عندما كنت صغيرة، قبل وقت ليس بالبعيد،
كنت مع أخي سامي وصديقاتي
نلعب على تراب لفحته الشمس.
كنا نضحك، نعدو عبر الصخور والرمل،
أحراراً كالطيور.

حين يعود أبي من الحقل،
يجلس لبعض الوقت تحت شجرة البرتقال
ويروي قصصاً عن أجدادنا.

In that not-so-distant memory
we were free.
Free to play, free to go to school.
Free to buy fruit and vegetables at the market.
Free to laugh and chat, drink tea with neighbors.
Always three cups.

But that was then.
And this is now.

في تلك الذكرى وهي ليست بعيدة
كنا أحراراً.
لنا حرية اللعب، وحرية الذهاب إلى المدرسة.
لنا حرية شراء الفواكه والخضراوات في السوق.
لنا حرية الضحك والدردشة، شرب الشاي مع الجيران.
ثلاثة أكواب دائماً.

كان هذا حينها،
وهذا ما يحدث الآن.

Back then Jedo, my grandfather, fished.
Papa worked in the fields.
Mama sewed silk scarves for me and my dolls.
Wrapped in silk and hugs,
I didn't know our lives would soon change
            forever.

في ذلك الحين كان جدي يصيد السمك.

أبي يعمل في الحقل.

أمي تخيط أوشحة حريرية لي ولدميتي.

يحيط بي الحرير والعناق.

لم أكن أعرف أن حياتنا ستتغير.

But Jedo said we weren't really free.
If we're not allowed to sing our songs,
to dance our dances,
to pray the prayers of our choice,
are we truly free?

لكن لجدي رأي آخر: لم نكن أحراراً في حقيقة الأمر.
إذا كنا لا نستطيع أن نغني أغانينا،
نرقص رقصاتنا،
نصلي الصلاة التي نختارها،
هل نحن حقاً أحرار؟

Then war came to our country.
Life in our village changed.
Nothing was as it had been.

Soon there was not enough food.
"Rama, share this bowl of soup with Sami."
I didn't know then that Mama would go hungry.

But we still had Mama's hugs,
and Jedo's arms to hold us.

بعدها جاءت الحرب إلى بلدي.

تغيّرت الحياة في قريتنا.

لم يبق شيء كما كان.

سرعان ما شحّ الطعام.

"راما، تقاسمي هذا الصحن من الشوربة مع سامي!"

لم أكن أعلم حينها أن أمي ستبقى جائعة.

لكننا بقينا نملك عناق ماما،

وذراعيّ جدي تطوقنا.

Then the birds stopped singing.
People began to leave our village.
First a trickle, then a stream,
across dusty fields under a burning sun,
a stream driven by hope.
Mothers, fathers, children,
seeking a better place, a better life.

بعدها توقفت الطيور عن الغناء.

بدأ الناس يغادرون قريتنا.

بدأوا فرادى ثم صاروا حشوداً،

يذهبون عبر حقول مغبرة تحت شمس حارقة،

تيارٌ يحركه الأمل.

أمهات، آباء، أطفال

يبحثون عن مكان أفضل، عن حياة أفضل.

A river of strangers in search of a place
to be free, to live and laugh, to love again.
In search of a place where bombs did not fall,
where people did not die on their way to market.
A river of people in search of peace.

نهر من الغرباء يبحث عن مكان،
عن الحرية، يريد الحياة والضحكة، الحب من جديد.
يبحث عن مكان لا تسقط عليه القنابل،
مكان لا يموت فيه الناس وهم ذاهبون للتسوق،
نهر من الناس يبحث عن السلام.

At first when our neighbors left, I didn't mind.
I had Papa and Mama and Jedo and Sami.
I still had friends.

We waved goodbye
not knowing they wouldn't come back.

But when bombs fell too close to our home,
Mama and Papa became frightened for us all.
I hid my face in Mama's lap and cried—
even though I am a big girl.

في البداية لم أهتم عندما غادر جيراننا.

كان لديّ بابا وماما وجدو وسامي.

لا يزال عندي صديقات.

لوّحنا لهم مودعين

دون أن نعلم أنهم لن يعودوا مرة أخرى.

ولكن عندما بدأت القنابل تسقط قريبة جداً من بيتنا،

بدأت أمي وأبي يخافان على سلامتنا.

أخفيت رأسي في حضن أمي وبكيت،

بالرغم من أنني فتاة كبيرة.

One day Jedo told Sami and me
that it was time.
Time to join the river of people,
time to leave all that we knew.

That night I lay in bed and cried
because I knew I would never again
hear the crow of the rooster, the creak of the gate,
the bleat of our goat.

I lay awake and listened to the wind,
wondering if the moon rises the same way
in other places.

ذات يوم أخبرني جدي أنا وسامي

أن الوقت قد حان

لنلتحق بنهر الناس،

لنترك كل ما نعرفه.

في تلك الليلة بكيت في فراشي

لأني كنت أعلم أنني لن أسمع صياح الديك مرة أخرى،

لن أسمع صرير البوابة

وثغاء العنزة.

تمددت دون أن أنام وأصغيت لصوت الريح،

وتساءلت هل يعلو القمر في الأماكن الأخرى كما يفعل هنا؟

Sami and I said goodbye to the flowers in our yard,
to our goat, to the soil we called home.

Then we walked.

We walked and walked and walked.
I tried to match my steps to Jedo's long strides.
I tried to hold Mama's hand,
but she carried blankets, a bundle of clothes.
I carried only memories in my heart.

أنا وسامي قلنا وداعاً للأزهار في حقلنا،

لعنزتنا، للتراب الذي نسميه البيت.

بعدها مشينا.

مشينا ومشينا ومشينا.

حاولت خطواتي أن تلحق بخطى جدي الواسعة.

حاولت أن أتشبث بيد أمي

لكنها كانت تحمل بطانيات وحزماً من الملابس.

لم أكن أحمل سوى الذكريات في قلبي.

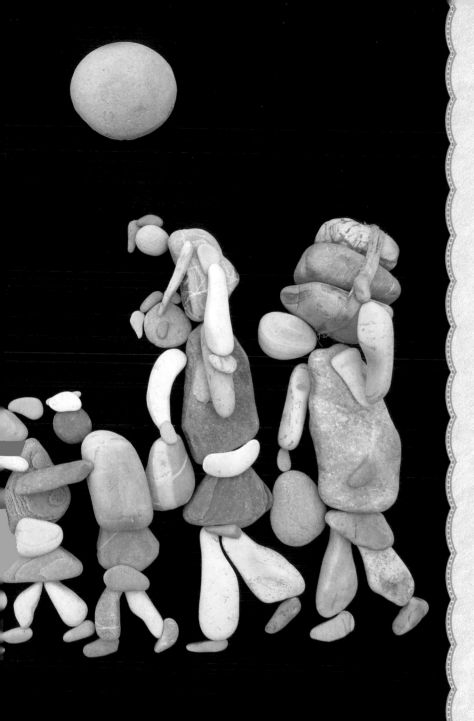

We walked,
sometimes alone but mostly with many others.
Everyone fleeing the war, running away
from the bombs.

Papa carried little Sami and more on his back.
When I grew so tired and cried,
Papa told me we were walking toward
a bright new future.

مشينا،
أحياناً لوحدنا ولكن معظم الوقت مع الكثير من الآخرين.
الكل يهرب من الحرب، ينجو بنفسه من القنابل.

كان أبي يحمل سامي الصغير وأشياء أخرى على ظهره.
عندما انتابني التعب بكيت
قال لي أبي إننا نمشي نحو مستقبل مشرق جديد.

We walked to the end of the earth.
And when we reached it, there was the sea.
We set sail on waves of hope and prayer.
I was frightened as the waves battered
our little boat.
And not everyone made it safely across.
We said prayers for those whose journey
ended at sea.

مشينا إلى نهاية العالم،

عندها وجدنا البحر.

أبحرنا على أمواج من الأمل والصلوات.

اعتراني الخوف لأن الأمواج ترتطم بزورقنا الصغير.

لم يتمكن أحد من العبور بسلام.

صلينا من أجل أولئك الذين انتهت رحلتهم في البحر.

When we arrived on land once again,
Mama and Papa planted seeds
to grow flowers
to remember those who did not
reach freedom.

عندما وصلنا اليابسة مرة أخرى،
زرع أبي وأمي بذوراً لتنمو الأزهار
ذكرى لأولئك الذين لم يصلوا إلى الحرية.

And on we walked.
Tired. I was so tired.
My feet felt like the rocks
        on which we walked.
My legs were trees, rooted to the soil.

On we walked.
But now we walked across lands
        free from war,
free from guns and bombs,
        free from fear.
Now we walked in hope.

ثم واصلنا المسير.

متعبين. كنت شديدة التعب.

شعرت أن قدميّ تشبهان الصخور التي نمشي عليها.

كانتا أشبه بالأشجار التي تمد جذورها في التراب.

واصلنا المسير.

لكننا بدأنا نمشي عبر أراض تخلو من الحرب،

تخلو من المدافع والقنابل، تخلو من الخوف.

الآن نمشي بأمل.

At last we came to our future.

New neighbors welcomed us with open arms.
I heard their voices but didn't understand
        their words.
But when I saw their smiles,
        I knew what the words meant.
"Stay!" they said.
"Stay here with us. You will be safe now.
No more war."

They shared what they had.
Clothes, food—even a new doll.

أخيراً وصلنا مستقبلنا.

استقبلنا جيران جدد بأذرع مفتوحة.
سمعت أصواتهم ولم أفهم كلماتهم.
لكني عندما رأيت ابتساماتهم، علمت معنى الكلمات.
قالوا: "امكثوا!
امكثوا هنا معنا. ستكونون بأمان الآن.
لا حرب بعد الآن."

تقاسموا معنا ما يمتلكون.
الملابس، الطعام ... وحتى دمية جديدة.

We have a new home now,
a home with new sounds and smells,
with smiles and people who help.
Will this always be home,
or will we go back one day?

صار لدينا بيت جديد الآن،
بيت فيه أصوات وروائح جديدة،
فيه ابتسامات وأناس يقدمون المساعدة.
أيكون هذا بيتنا دائماً
أم سنعود ذات يوم؟

The lucky ones, they call us.
New memories, new hopes,
    new dreams.
Not of war,
but of peace.

يسموننا المحظوظون.
ذكريات جديدة، أمال جديدة، أحلام جديدة.
ليس عن الحرب،
بل عن السلام.

MARGRIET RUURS is the author of many award-winning books for children. She was inspired to write *Stepping Stones* after she stumbled across the amazing stone artwork of Nizar Ali Badr on the Internet and saw the opportunity to both raise funds to help Syrian refugees and bring the work of Mr. Badr to a wider audience. Margriet enjoys speaking about reading and writing to students at schools around the world. Her adventures have taken her to such countries as Myanmar, Pakistan, Laos, Tanzania and many others. Margriet was born in The Netherlands but has been a Canadian for most of her life. She lives with her family on Salt Spring Island, British Columbia.

NIZAR ALI BADR was born and still resides in Latakia, Syria. Living in one of the oldest civilizations on Earth, he has always been inspired to paint, sculpt and draw. In his walks along the seashore near the ancient port city of Ugarit, he always admired the stones on the beach and in the clear blue water. Now he gathers these stones and brings them home to his rooftop studio, where they become the medium for his art. These works in stone display a remarkable narrative quality, some based on the legends and tales told to him by his grandmother, others more contemporary in nature.

An experienced sculptor, Nizar has never left his hometown or his country, though in his heart he accompanies the many Syrians who have been forced to flee their homeland because of ongoing violence.

What can you do to make a difference?

Here are a number of links you may wish to explore.

- **Canadian Council for Refugees** (www.ccrweb.ca)

  After you visit this site, contact a local group to see how you and your family can help.

- **American Refugee Committee** (www.arcrelief.org)
- **United Nations Refugee Agency** (www.unhcr.ca)

  Coordinates UN refugee responses, including support for host countries providing assistance for Syrian refugees.

- **Unicef Canada** (www.unicef.ca)

  The United Nations Children's Fund is a child-focused humanitarian organization operating in 192 countries, including Syria.

- **Doctors Without Borders** (www.doctorswithoutborders.org)

  Operates medical facilities inside Syria and supports more than 100 clinics, health posts and field hospitals in the country.

- **International Rescue Committee** (www.rescue.org)
- **Oxfam** (www.oxfam.org)

  An international confederation of seventeen organizations working around the world to find solutions to poverty and to support human rights.

- **Canadian Red Cross** (www.redcross.ca)

  Part of the international humanitarian organization, the Red Cross is helping to support the efforts of the Syrian Arab Red Crescent in Syria.

A portion of the proceeds from the sale of this book will be donated to resettlement organizations across North America. For more information visit **www.steppingstonesthebook.com**.